Oxford University Press, Walton Street, Oxford OX2 6DP

Oxford New York Toronto
Petaling Jaya Singapore Hong Kong Tokyo
Delhi Bombay Calcutta Madras Karachi
Nairobi Dar es Salaam Cape Town
Melbourne Auckland

and associated companies in
Berlin Ibadan

Oxford is a trade mark of Oxford University Press

Illustrations © Korky Paul 1989
Text © Peter Carter 1989

First published 1989 Reprinted 1990

British Library Cataloguing in Publication Data
Carter, Peter, 1929–
    Captain Teachum's buried treasure.
    I. Title   II. Paul Korky
    823'.914[J]
ISBN 0–19–279869–3

Printed in Hong Kong

For Zoë: KP

Captain Teachum's BURIED TREASURE

Korky Paul and Peter Carter

Oxford University Press

Oxford Toronto Melbourne

Captain Teachum was a pirate.
He said.
He was the wickedest pirate
in the world—he said.

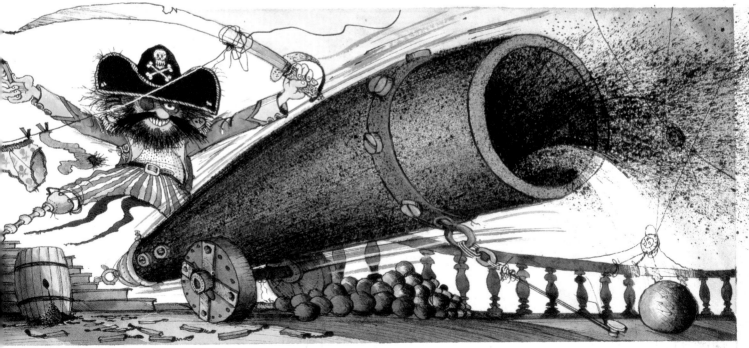

He attacked castles.

He captured ships.

He burned down whole towns.

And he made people walk the plank—he said.
He was the terror of the seven seas.

He buried his treasure.
He said.
He buried his treasure in ruined castles.

He buried his treasure
on desert islands.

Sinus Nauseabundus

TATIUM

Promontorium Dentium Falsium

He buried it in jungles—he said.

He buried it in the South Pole.
He buried it all over the world—he said.

He buried it in the North Pole.

But Captain Teachum had three secrets.
His wife made him do the washing-up!

He had *twenty-five* children!
And he had an awful memory, so . . .

He couldn't remember where he had buried his treasure!
He looked everywhere.
In the ruined castles,
on the desert islands,
in the jungles,
at the North Pole and at the South Pole.
But he couldn't find it anywhere!
So . . .

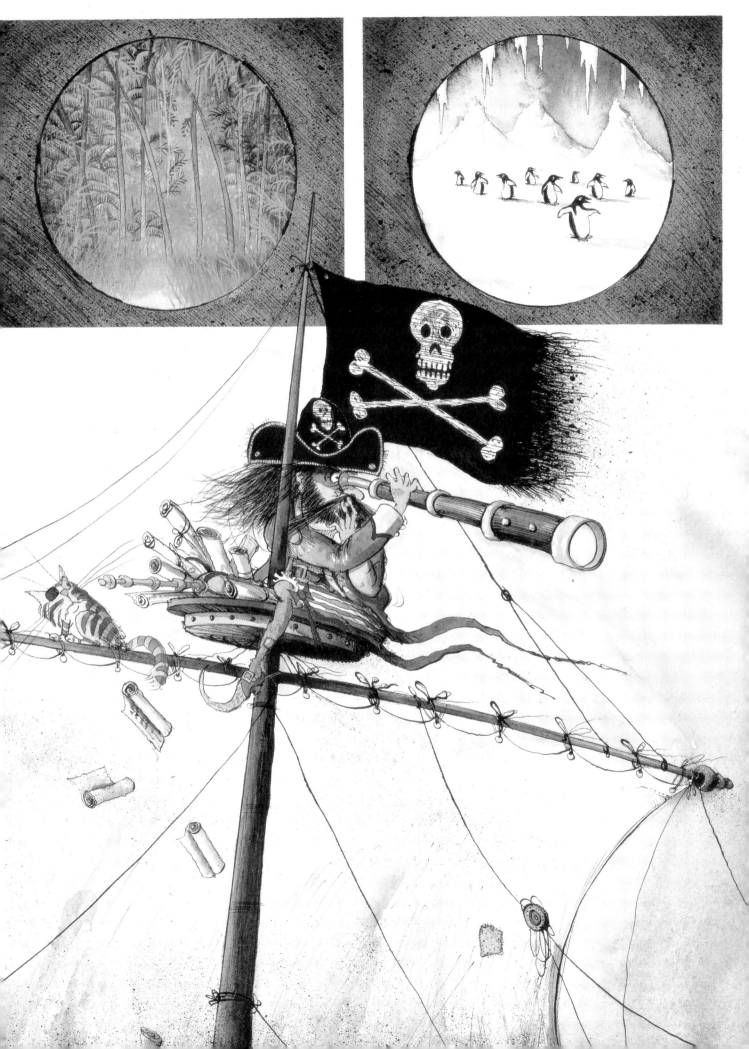

Maybe the treasure is still there.
Maybe . . .
He said.